HEDGEHOG WHODUNIT

Written by Heather Preusser

Art by Gal Weizman

Andrews McMeel
PUBLISHING®

HEDGEHOG WHODUNIT

© 2024 Heather Preusser. Illustrations by Gal Weizman. All rights reserved. Printed in China. No part of this book may be used or reproduced in any manner whatsoever without written permission except in the case of reprints in the context of reviews.

Andrews McMeel Publishing
a division of Andrews McMeel Universal
1130 Walnut Street, Kansas City, Missouri 64106
www.andrewsmcmeel.com

24 25 26 27 28 SDB 10 9 8 7 6 5 4 3 2 1

Paperback ISBN: 978-1-5248-8252-5

Hardcover ISBN: 978-1-5248-9400-9

Library of Congress Control Number: 2024935831

Editor: Erinn Pascal
Art Director: Diane Marsh
Production Manager: Jeff Preuss
Production Editor: Dave Shaw

Made by:
RR Donnelley (Guangdong) Printing Solutions Company Ltd
Address and location of manufacturer:
No. 2, Minzhu Road, Daning, Humen Town,
Dongguan City, Guangdong Province, China 523930
1st Printing—6/03/24

ATTENTION: SCHOOLS AND BUSINESSES
Andrews McMeel books are available at quantity discounts with bulk purchase for educational, business, or sales promotional use. For information, please e-mail the Andrews McMeel Publishing Special Sales Department: sales@amuniversal.com.

CHAPTER 1

I've heard it all before: Hedgehogs don't hunt down hooligans. In fact, we have a reputation for not doing much of anything, which is baloney. Not that I eat baloney. Let me set the record straight.

Name's Hitch

I'm a sharp-witted hedgehog detective. I keep this joint safe by putting culprits behind bars. (Most likely they're already behind bars. After all, this is a zoo.)

I was curled up in the **Hedgehog Hut** when my sidekick, a scraggly, wire-haired rodent named Vinnie, barged in. Since he has free run of the zoo, he gives me the skinny on all the animals' comings and goings. In exchange, I keep him out of trouble.

That's **Vinnie**

The Informer

"Feeling prickly today, boss?" Vinnie asked.

"Well, yes," I replied. I have six thousand spines covering my back; I am always prickly. "I was just about to take my **mid-evening nap.**"

"No time for naps," Vinnie said, chewing his own greasy, pink tail. (He claimed it helped him concentrate.) "We're in a pickle, which sounds delicious right about now, especially on top of a big, juicy cheeseburger with a side of hand-cut fries and some brown sugar BBQ ketchup. Lots and lots of ketchup."

Vinnie dropped his tail and scampered back and forth like one of those exhausting windup toys going nowhere that kids always leave behind.

I closed my eyes. Although a cheeseburger and fries sounded tempting, I was more into insects.

"But that's not why I'm here," Vinnie continued, snapping out of his food-induced daydream. "I'm here because **there's a mystery afoot!** Someone changed the sign in the panda exhibit. It used to say, "PLEASE DON'T FEED THE PANDA." Now it says, "PLEASE free THE PANDA," and that giant bear is nowhere to be seen!"

Vinnie took a deep breath. "All I found was this list of ingredients someone left behind."

I opened one eyelid. "What list?" I asked.

Vinnie rubbed his belly and **belched.** "The one I ate," he replied.

"Gross," I said. "Well, pandas aren't in my jurisdiction."

I deal with domestic cases, and by "domestic," I mean cases I can solve from the comfort of my homey hedge. I am the perfect P.I., but more of a P.P.I., a *Private* Private Investigator. I only ever leave my leafy nest to forage for more food. Plus, I solved my most recent case last year when we pinned down a parrot sending mean notes (he wanted more crackers). "I've already met my quota for solving cases."

CHAPTER 1

"The perpetrators are still on the loose," said Vinnie. "It could be hours, days, or weeks before we're able to track them down. The longer it takes to pinpoint those pranksters, the more signs they'll likely vandalize, which could mean **more** missing mammals, **more** disorder, **more** disarray, **more** disturbances! IT'LL TURN INTO A ZOO AROUND HERE!"

"Well, yes," I replied. "The City Zoo, to be exact."

"Plus, a panda on the prowl will surely cause a *panda*-monium! Which means no more long spontaneous grooming sessions and no shut-eye for you."

That spiked my interest. I opened my other eyelid. "Wait, did you say 'no shut-eye'?"

"Affirmative, boss," said Vinnie. "That's exactly what I said, which is a problem because you need your eighteen hours of beauty sleep every day."

I thought of raising one of my toes in objection. Eighteen hours of sleep is laughable. I needed at least twenty or else I become a first-class grump.

If I wanted any peace and quiet anytime soon, I'd have to get Vinnie off my back by tracking down that bamboo-loving bear and those sign-changing hooligans. And I'd have to do it tonight. If the panda wasn't properly returned to his pen

before The City Zoo reopened tomorrow, the zookeepers would certainly sound the alarm.

I sighed. A nap would have to wait. "Okay, I'll take the case. After, I *nap.*"

EHOG WHODUNIT TURF — DO NO

CHAPTER 2

Step one to solve a case: take stock of supplies.

Vinnie was busy taking inventory and testing out his spy equipment. A gadgeteer, he was always collecting random stuff—mostly broken—and then storing it in his vault.

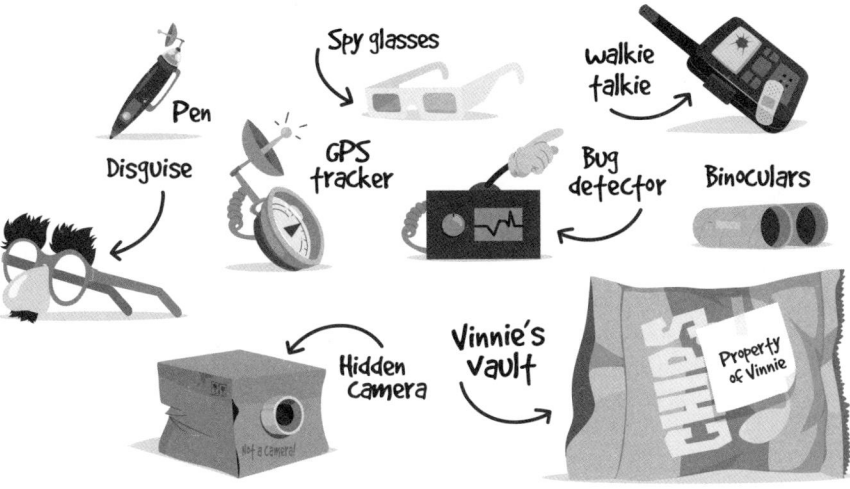

"Voice-activated recorder pen?" Vinnie said. "**Aye.** GPS tracker? **Aye.** Hidden camera? **Aye.** Walkie-talkie, spy glasses, and bug detector? **Aye aye,** captain!"

"Why do you sound like a seadog?" I asked.

"My voice-activated pen is on the fritz," Vinnie said. "Now it only activates if I talk like a pirate."

Shiver me timbers, I thought. This was going to be a long case.

"Vinnie, what was on that list of ingredients you ate earlier?" We needed to get to the bottom of this case, and—so far—that was our only clue.

"I only remember the first item," Vinnie replied. "**Fish.**"

"Well, there are a lot of fish-eating animals in these parts," I began. "Where do we start?"

"I have an idea," Vinnie said with his nose in the air. "Do you smell that, boss?"

"Thought it was you," I replied.

"Not this time." He followed the scent out the office. "It's coming from the penguins in the **Southern Shores** exhibit. That could be the fish we're looking for! And my next snack!"

Then the varmit took off before I even responded. I had to give it to the rodent: He was quick. I, on the other hand, am more of a meanderer, averaging about three and a half miles per hour (four if I'm feeling rambunctious, but I wasn't).

The thought of socializing with the penguins made my skin **crawl.** Not like that's too hard to do (at least one hundred fleas hang out there all the time). But I poked my way to the Southern Shores exhibit anyway.

By the time I approached the penguins, Vinnie had marked off the area with yellow crime-scene tape that read, "**HEDGEHOG WHODUNIT TURF—DO NOT CROSS,**" and he was busy licking brown powder off every surface.

"Just dusting for fingerprints, pawprints, and wingprints, boss," he explained. "Haven't found any yet."

We often searched for fingerprints by sprinkling powder and then dusting it off with a brush.

CHAPTER 2

"Since when do you dust with your tongue?" I asked.

"Since I ran out of adhesive powder and had to use hot cocoa," he replied, attempting to clean the powder off his whiskers. "And it's **delish.** It'd go great with a salty pairing, like a soft pretzel, or maybe some spiced, roasted almonds and toasted pumpkin seeds—but only if the pumpkin seeds are drizzled with Worcestershire sauce."

"Wu-stuh-what?" I asked.

"Wu-stuh-SURE," Vinnie repeated.

"Easier done than said," I replied. I put on my glasses to get a better look at the sign above the penguins' pool. It had been changed. It used to say "PLEASE THROW TRASH AWAY," but someone had crossed out the last two words and a new word was written below in red paint. Now it read: "PLEASE THROW Sardines."

CHAPTER 2

"Looks fishy," said Vinnie. "I bet it's a red herring."

"Sardines aren't herring," I clarified, "although they are in that fish family." (Plus, a red herring, which is a clue intended to mislead or distract a detective, never fooled this sleuth-hog.) "And no eating the evidence," I added, prying a sardine out of Vinnie's paw.

I tossed the small fish over my shoulder. One nearby penguin called **"heads."** Another called **"tails."**

I eyed Vinnie suspiciously. "Hand them *all* over," I said.

Vinnie gave me a smarmy smile. "*Sardine*ly, boss," he said, surrendering the bucket of bait hidden behind his back.

Vinnie turned to me. "Aren't you going talk to the penguin pair?" he asked.

I eyed the penguin couple perched atop the fake glacier. With their flippers now crossed in front of their chests, they appeared to study the lay of the land. I bet they knew something about that list of ingredients or the altered signs. "Of course," I replied. Nothing like some good ol' bait for a good ol' bribe . . .

As I made my way to the penguin pair, a sardine thwacked me on the noggin. I slipped and tripped on another as I passed the artificial igloo. A third stuck in my spines before I curled into a protective ball.

CHAPTER 2

"Perhaps it would be bene*fish*ial if I took the lead, boss?" asked Vinnie. "I'll do the interrogation. Stand by for **Operation Hook, Line, and Stinker!**"

"**Ahoy, mateys!**" Vinnie said to the penguin pair. "Where were **ye** this morning? Were **ye** making a list of ingredients? Know anyone who had it in for that giant panda, anyone who'd want to give him a good **keelhauling?** What can **ye** tell us about that sign so we don't have to **feed ye to the fish?** Speaking of fish, which do **ye** prefer: roasted sardines with seaweed salsa verde or herring curry salad with a splash of mayonnaise?"

"Vinnie, stay focused," I insisted.

"Right, boss." Vinnie turned his attention back to the duo who seemed to digest the bucket of bait with their eyes.

"Are you that hedgehog detective?" one penguin asked me.

I nodded, flashing my shiny sleuthing badge.

"We've just been here chilling, listening to music," the penguin continued, pointing to the headphones perched atop his pint-sized noggin. I tried to ignore the sounds of **"Arctic Funk"** assailing my ears. "We heard that panda dude was cooking up trouble," said the other penguin, "but we don't know anything about it."

"Sounds like bunk," I said (which is detective lingo for **"nonsense"**). "Here's what I heard: Two zoo signs have been changed, there's no trace of that missing bear, and there're no fingerprints, pawprints, or wingprints anywhere—"

CHAPTER 2

"Which suggests the criminal act was premeditated," interrupted Vinnie. "It was planned ahead of time. And **the red paint is still wet.**"

"Which tells me the crime was done less than an hour ago," I said.

"And," continued Vinnie, "the drips on the sign show it was painted in a rush." He leaned in closer to the penguins, pointing his pen at them as if applying pressure. "Any idea who's behind it, **buccaneers?**"

"What's criminal about having a tasty treat?" asked one of the penguins.

"Criminal act number one: **SELFISHNESS.** You didn't share those treats with me," said Vinnie.

"Criminal act number two: **VANDALISM,**" I said.

"That's right," added Vinnie. "Zoo property has been destroyed. And criminal act number three: **THEFT.**" He paused, twirling his whiskers for effect. "Where did all those sardines come from anyway?"

"No clue," said the penguin's partner. "We just perform adorable acts and they appear. Check it out." She teetered to the edge of the pool and executed a full-feathered summersault with no splash. When she rocketed to the water's surface, a sardine flew over the fence.

"There's more where that came from," I said, holding out the bucket of bait with one hand. "They're yours for the taking if you tell us what you know about who's behind that sign."

"What's it *guano* be?" asked Vinnie, tapping the pen against his notepad.

CHAPTER 2

I was too tired to comment on Vinnie's poop pun. (Guano is *not* detective lingo. It means **poop,** particularly **seabird poop.**)

One penguin put a flipper on a fish. "Check out those hippo dudes," he said. "They're dangerous, aggressive, and unpredictable."

"Yeah, they're a *ton* of trouble," Vinnie added, writing the hippos down as suspects.

I wrote the penguins off as flightless, shameless birds who would do anything for a few fish. "We'll get to the bottom of this," I said. "After I catch some **mid-evening post-dinner pre-bedtime shut-eye.**"

CHAPTER 3

As I was relaxing, Vinnie rolled a television monitor into the office.

"Vinnie, we're in the middle of a case," I said. "There's no time to watch the cooking channel. We need to pump those hippos for information."

"It's not the cooking channel. It's video surveillance from a camera I hid in a trashcan near your hut. Now you can locate the panda and find the yahoos who changed the two signs from the comfort of your own home."

No argument there.

Vinnie turned on the television, but it only displayed static. He **smacked** the monitor

again and **again** and **again.** "This measly machine doesn't work!"

Of course it didn't work. That rat broke spy gear faster than he inhaled twice-baked macaroni and cheese.

He unplugged it and then plugged it back in. A close-up of a curious squirrel froze on the screen. "I think this bushy tail is moving in on our turf, boss," Vinnie continued.

"Looks like he's moving in on those leftover hotdogs," I replied.

"Those are my tasty meat trimmings!"

"Wait a **hot-hedgehog minute!**" I said, peering at the screen. "Is that a whistling panda with a cast-iron pan in the background?" We needed to get a move on. "What do you say, time to make our next visit?" I asked Vinnie.

"Follow me, boss!" he replied.

I followed Vinnie's distinct rotten rat smell to the trashcan with the hidden camera. There were no signs of the **pan-toting panda** or the **tasty meat trimmings.**

When we arrived at the hippos' home, Vinnie started taking pictures from every angle as the hippos basked in the midday sun.

"Just capturing the evidence, boss," Vinnie said. He crouched and zoomed in on a large hippo grazing in the grass, but each time he pressed the shutter button, the camera merely played circus music.

"Not another gadget from Vinnie's Vault," I said, pocketing the malfunctioning camera.

Another hippo and her calf moseyed by. "**Smile!**" said the hippo calf, and Vinnie posed for a photo, first with the hippo's camera, then the calf's, and then the hippo's again because Vinnie couldn't hold still.

"It's a hippo*party*mus in here," said Vinnie.

"**Cannonball!**" shouted another hippo, jumping in a pool of mud and sending slop everywhere.

"Make that a hippopota*mess*," Vinnie corrected.

"I'm guessing it has to do with the new sign," I remarked. I polished my glasses and pointed above Vinnie's head. With the same drippy, red paint we saw in the penguins' pool, someone had crossed out the sign that used to say "SPRAY ZONE." Now it read "Selfie ZONE," and hippos were busy taking snapshots of themselves and posing for pictures with other hippos.

I did some mental math. That made three changed signs and one missing mammal. We had to find the culprits soon before everything went south.

I approached the hippo who was clearly in charge—she was calling all the shots—with the biggest HipPro camera mounted on her helmet.

"Nice weather," I said. "Perfect for capturing a few candid shots." I cut right to the chase. "Know anything about that sign or a panda on the loose?"

"Sign?" the head honcho repeated. "We've been busy soaking in the spotlight. Say 'cheese'!"

We all smiled for the camera.

"What I wouldn't give for some delicious cheese right now," said Vinnie. "With salami and prosciutto and those perfectly round crackers with fig jam and fresh grapes. And you can't forget the marinated olives—preferably the ones without the pits. Just hand me an apron, and I'll start slicing and dicing."

CHAPTER 3

"Now that you mention it," said the hippo, "I did see a panda singing in an apron earlier today."

"Which way was the panda headed?" I asked.

But the hippo was busy gathering her loud herd. "**Group photo!**" she announced.

"I'll sit this one out," I said, slinking to the side. Although the camera loved my cute face, the mere mention of a group made me curl up in fear.

On the ground under a hippo hoof was our next clue: a piece of paper. But I could only make out the first two words. It read: "CALLING AL . . ."

"Who's AL?" I asked the head honcho hippo when the photo op was over.

"Just a fan," she said, kicking the sheet aside with her hind hoof.

"You hippos are pretty popular these days," Vinnie said. "You're **practically famous.**"

I wasn't buying the bit about fan mail, but a good hedgehog detective knows when to play along. "Can we have your autograph?" I asked her.

She blushed. "I'd be happy to."

Vinnie handed over his notepad.

The hippo dipped one of her front hooves in a mud puddle and stamped a blank page.

Vinnie and I scrutinized the results.

It was a hoofprint, and the changed signs were handwritten. We were barking up the wrong tree. Not that I can bark. (I've been told I have an **adorable** snort.)

"Prepare for **Operation Claim to Fame,**" Vinnie whispered to me. Then he turned to the hippo. "We can help rocket you to stardom. One press of a button and I can share that photo on **RATCHAT, CRITTERGRAM,** and **MUGBOOK.**"

CHAPTER 3

The hippo clapped her front hooves.

"But fame comes at a price," Vinnie continued. Now he was playing hardball. "Tell us what you know about who's behind that sign, and you'll be a social media sensation in seconds."

I had to hand it to Vinnie: The rodent didn't have a moral fiber on that scruffy, scrappy body of his, but he sure knew how to get the job done.

"Try the lions," the hippo said without missing a beat. "They're pals with the panda."

"Yeah, their pride often leads them down the wrong path," Vinnie said. He hit "**SHARE**," the photo went viral, and we added the lions to our list of suspects.

I stopped a shady looking hippo on our way out. "Can I borrow your sunglasses?" I asked. "They're perfect for catching some Zs."

GEHOG WHODUNIT TURF — DO NOT

CHAPTER 4

I needled through the clues so far:

Clue #1: Someone altered the signs in the Panda Palace, Penguins' Pool, and Hippos' Home.

Clue #2: The panda was missing-in-action, aka MIA.

Clue #3: Vinnie discovered a list of ingredients in the panda's pen. (I had to take Vinnie's word on this one since he ate the evidence.)

Clue #4: The penguins reported rumors of the panda cooking up trouble.

Clue #5: Vinnie's video surveillance caught a whistling panda with a pan lurking around.

Clue #6: The head honcho hippo claimed she saw a singing panda in an apron.

Clue #7: The hippos were supposedly getting fan mail from someone named AL.

Just as I was boiling down the case, dance music started blaring. It was ruffling my feathers. Not that I have feathers.

I wiped the almost-sleep from my eyes. "What's the 1-1-4?" I asked.

"You mean the 4-1-1?" Vinnie replied.

Clearly, I needed some shut-eye. I felt like I hadn't slept in minutes.

Vinnie put down his elaborate diagrams. "According to the hippos, there's an uproar in the lions' lair, so I've been devising a foolproof plan for breaking and entering. I call it **Operation Meal Deal.**" He pointed to the nearest chart. "If we dig a tunnel under Bird World, we'll arrive at **Predator Ridge** just in time for lunch. We'll drill a hole into

CHAPTER 4

the lions' den, and all those scrumptious beef shish kabobs meant for those lazy wildcats will be ours for the taking! Add a grilled zucchini salad with a sprinkling of lemon and scallions as well as some tangy red cabbage slaw, and we have ourselves a meal!" He was so excited, his fur stood on end as if he'd been hanging out under one of those restroom hand dryers..

"There's only one problem with your foolproof plan," I began.

Vinnie's fur slumped.

"It doesn't get us any closer to solving the case." Plus, we could end up as hedgehog-and-rat kabobs before the job was done.

Vinnie went back to the **drawing board.** Literally. He scribbled here and there, crumpled up a few charts, ate them, burped, and scratched out some more sketches. "You have great nighttime vision. What if we slide down a rope from the roof in the dark of night? Or we can crawl through the ventilation system. Or I can create a diversion by setting up a karaoke machine. My rendition of 'The Lion Sleeps Tonight' is arresting, particularly if I add dance moves—you could join in on the chorus!"

CHAPTER 4

"Or we can just enter through the gate," I said.

"Fine," said Vinnie, "but where's the **adventure,** the **peril,** the **living-on-the-hedge lifestyle?!**"

"I'm a hedgehog," I reminded him. "I'm always living on the hedge."

At the lions' lair, Vinnie completed a chalk outline of each and every lion as they lazed about.

"Doesn't look like much of a crime scene to me," I said. I cleaned my glasses. I didn't see any sign of foul play and none of the signs had been altered.

"You're right. They're all just *lion* around," added Vinnie.

I couldn't make heads or tails of the situation. Not that I have much of a tail.

We approached a lion and a lioness who were giving each other a bath. "Know anything about this black-and-white galoot?" I asked, holding up a photograph of the panda.

The lion stopped licking. "Personally, I'm partial to rats, especially greasy ones—they go down easier."

Vinnie was at a loss for words, which never happens. I attempted to change the subject. "Know anything about someone named AL or the signs around the zoo?" I asked.

"You mean like that sign there?"

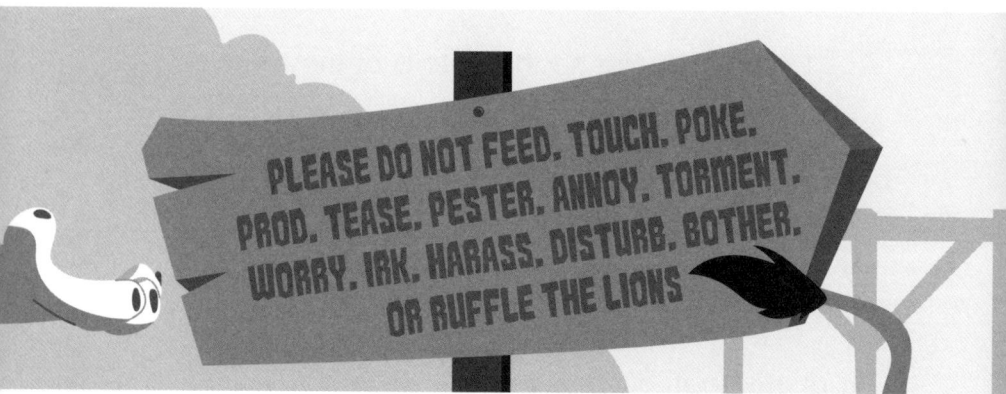

"It should also say, 'DO NOT INTERRUPT LIONS WHILE BATHING.'"

I had to give it to him for appreciating a good grooming routine. I, too, liked a good rub or roll every now and then.

He cleaned each and every claw until they gleamed.

Vinnie was so nervous he climbed onto my back and appeared to be rooting through my spines for a snack. He nudged me between bites. "Maybe the hippos were lying."

"Maybe we just need to do more sleuthing," I said, inching away from the cat couple.

We slunk out of Predator Ridge and closed the gate behind us.

"I've got it," whispered Vinnie. "Let's arrange a stakeout. We'll rent a car with tinted windows, scope out the neighborhood, and eat pizza while we're on **panda patrol.**"

GEHOG WHODUNIT TURF — DO NO

CHAPTER 5

Stakeout

From our high vantage point, I spotted something out of the ordinary.

"Vinnie, look!" I pointed to two lemurs carrying a bucket of red paint below. I had a hunch it was the same paint we saw on the signs at the penguins' pool and the hippos' home.

"Those are our culprits!" said Vinnie. "And they're making a **clean sneak!**"

That's code, which means the miscreant lemurs were escaping without leaving a trace. I had to get my ducks in a row. Not that I know any ducks (at least not well-organized ones).

We just had to lock up the lemurs, pin down the panda, change the signs back to the way they were, and I could rejoice in peace and quiet with a well-earned nap. I could almost imagine it now . . .

"Targets are on the move!" cried Vinnie.

"Abandon Operation Stakeout Takeout!" I ordered. "I repeat, **abandon Operation Stakeout Takeout!**"

"Copy that!"

I left my post and followed Vinnie away from the lions and through the Woodland Garden. Finally, we made it to the Snack Shack. **Almost.**

CHAPTER 5

Vinnie slid on something, his feet flew in the air, and his arms flailed about. He landed on his back with a **thud.** "It appears we're in a slippery situation, boss."

The ground was covered in a mysterious slick substance. The goop looked like small marbles, which meant it wasn't produced by anything big; it was odorless, which meant it wasn't Vinnie's doing since anything associated with him reeks; and it appeared to be localized to this area, which meant we were simply in the wrong place at the wrong time. My **hedgie senses** were **activated,** but further investigation wasn't worth my time—mainly because I didn't have more time to spare. For reasons I couldn't fully explain, I had the urge to stop and cover myself with foamy saliva.

Right then and there. It was like having an itch I had to scratch, only I wasn't itchy or scratchy. Instead, I was foaming at the mouth and contorting my body in various positions, trying to spread my spittle on every inch of my spines.

"Wait, boss, are you grooming now?" asked Vinnie.

"Don't mind me," I said. "I just need to lick my spines. **Right away.**"

"But we'll lose the lemurs' trail!"

And he was right. For once.

"A self-anointing hedgehog has to do what a self-anointing hedgehog has to do," I said.

"Self-anointing?" said Vinnie. "Sounds like you're appointing yourself knight, or king, or something important."

"I'm already important," I replied, my mouth full of froth. Using my tongue, I spread the froth on my quills. "Now I'll be important *and* clean."

That's what self-anointing is all about: **cleanliness**

(and perhaps a bit of camouflage and self-protection). At least, that's what this detective has deduced. Why I feel the urge to self-anoint is one mystery I've never been able to solve.

By the time I had slicked my spines—all six thousand of them—with saliva, the lemurs were long gone, and the rat was busy collecting samples.

"I'm just **tagging, logging,** and **packaging** this goop I slipped in for the forensics lab," Vinnie said. "Then I thought I'd get a mouth swab of every animal that's been in the vicinity in the last twenty-four hours. We can cross-check it with the activity from the hidden camera in the hot dog stand and see if that gives us any leads on who made this mess."

"Or we can simply **look up,**" I said, pointing to the flock of pigeons flying overhead. Since the pigeons weren't part of any zoo exhibit, they were free birds. Literally. "Looks like this isn't goop but poop." Pigeon poop to be precise.

One bird cooed as if in agreement and then pooped again. **Right. On. My. Head.**

I was prone to covering myself in my own poop, but this was simply preposterous!

"What a stinker," said Vinnie. "That gutter bird got you good."

Before I could respond, we were being chased by **a squadron of pooping pigeons.**

I ducked right, and they did their duty right.

I dodged left, and they defecated left.

CHAPTER 5

I slipped and slid until I was curled up in a ball on the pavement, doused in dung.

Vinnie rolled on the ground with laughter. "You alright there, boss? You look a little woozy. **Pooped,** even."

I was too pooped to comment on Vinnie's vile puns. Or clean the pigeon poop that added to my rough-around-the-hedges appearance. My gorgeous groom was gone!

"I'm so exhausted I'm seeing stars," I said. I was imagining one minute of blissful sleepy solitude when, from my new vantage point, I eyed something splattered on the pavement. "Only those don't look like stars."

"No, those look more like drops," said Vinnie. "Red drops."

Wait a **hot-hedgehog minute!**

I wasn't seeing stars. I was seeing **clues**—right under my nose!

"Look," said Vinnie, sniffing the evidence. "They start here on the other side of the Snack Shack and continue into the Lemur Lounge." He smeared a drop with one of his hands. "And these drops fell recently from a bucket of paint, which means we're hot on our villains' tails!"

Not exactly. By my calculations—and thanks to my predilection for grooming and the platoon of pooping pigeons—our villains had at least an hour's head start on us.

Vinnie took out his cracked magnifying glass. "It's time to bag this baddie and commence **Operation Paint the Town Red!**"

We followed the red paint drops around Zookeeper Zone, where young visitors learn to feed, maintain, and clean the animals. As we circled the zoo's carousel, Vinnie's ears perked up. "Hear that, boss?" he asked.

Of course I heard it. I felt it too. It was dance music in the distance, and the bass was so loud the ground had a heartbeat. It was coming from the direction of the Lemur Lounge.

"I suspect a **conspiracy** with those lemurs," said Vinnie.

"Well, yes," I replied. "That's what you call a group of lemurs." I wasn't hedging my bets. My money was on the lemurs too. Not that I have use for money.

EHOG WHODUNIT TURF — DO NO

CHAPTER 6

Vinnie pulled out his flashlight. Each time he tried turning it on, it shocked him and he shrieked. Every. Single. Time.

We followed what we could see of the paint trail in the lamplight, and two shakes of Vinnie's shocked tail later, we were at the lemurs' digs. The sign that used to say "**ZOOKEEPER SAYS: 'STAY BACK'**" now said "**ZOOKEEPER SAYS: Dance!**" I ran the numbers: **four** altered signs, **one** missing panda, **two** disgruntled lions, and **one long** overdue nap.

"Well, I'll be a monkey's uncle," said Vinnie.

Three monkeys swung from the disco ball hanging overhead.

"I'm sure he's been invited to this dance party as well," I said. Along with the rest of the monkey's family tree. And most of the other animals.

It really was, well, a **zoo.**

Everyone who was anyone was there, including the hippos and penguins.

CHAPTER 6

I didn't want to step closer to the hobnobbing, so I turned to Vinnie. "What do you say we call it a day?" I asked. "It's a jungle in there. Literally. Better to come back tomorrow after I've—we've—regrouped and recharged. Alone."

But the scatterbrained rascal was already running toward the food. "Boss, do you see what I see?"

I saw a flamingo attempting the moonwalk.

I imagined that I saw a panda's paw carrying a tray of food. I was so tired I must have been seeing things.

"Look at all the dance-party dishes!" Vinnie cried, reaching for another tray. "I've been eying these delightful pigs in a blanket!"

Three pigs who were dressed in togas made from blankets glared at Vinnie as they formed a conga line and 1-2-3 kicked their way to the dance floor.

"I just ate the lion's share of a jalapeno cheese ball," Vinnie said between bites, "and I even saw those cute cucumber sandwiches with the crust cut off. You know, the triangular ones?"

CHAPTER 6

"Did you say 'lion's share'?" I asked.

"**Mmmf**," he replied while chewing on some mozzarella sticks.

"No more eating the evidence," I said, plucking the sticks from Vinnie's mouth. "Haven't you noticed an absence?"

"Well, now that you mention it, boss, a nice marinara sauce would go well with those mozzarella sticks." He licked the grease off his forepaws.

"Not some*thing*, some*one*," I said.

Still nothing.

"Don't you find it odd no one bothered inviting the king of the jungle and his royal cohorts to the year's wildest dance party?" I asked.

"Perhaps lions can't dance because they have two left feet," suggested Vinnie.

They also have two right feet, but who's counting?

"No, something's up," I said, and it wasn't just the flying squirrels overhead. I adjusted my glasses and spotted a ring-tailed lemur with a distinctive striped tail. With her proud posture, she sure looked important. She was our ringleader. "It's time to interrogate the lemurs."

"Okay," said Vinnie, "but this mission needs a code name. How about **Operation Lemurgency?**"

"You've done better," I said. We started approaching the troop's leader.

CHAPTER 6

"How about **Operation Prime Time** or **Operation Three-Ring Circus?**" Vinnie added.

"I like the last one," I said. "It has a nice ring to it."

Just as we were closing in, the ring-tail leader let out a **loud, alarming** call that sounded like a cross between a growl and a bark. I think it loosened a few of my teeth.

As if on cue, her nearby ring-tail associates came running. They raised their smelly, bushy tails and shook them at us, starting a stink fight. Then they hightailed it out of there.

"**Follow that foul stench!**" I ordered. I rolled into a ball, and Vinnie gave me a push.

The ring-tails raised a stink around the dance floor, and I continued rolling. They gave us the stink eye from the drink table, and I gained speed, rocking right into Vinnie, who had paused for some punch. I knocked him off his feet, and he stuck to my spines. We reeled around the buffet, bumping into lemurs left and right. Each lemur latched on. We were all rolled into one big ball until we careened into the dessert table and came to a stop.

We untangled ourselves, and Vinnie helped himself to a few doughnuts stuck in my spines.

The lemurs lumped together as if huddling for a post-stink-fight debrief.

"You win," I said to our number one suspects. "You can stop the stink stance."

The lemurs lowered their tails, rubbing them back and forth between the scent glands on their

CHAPTER 6

wrists. I had to act fast, especially if I wanted to stop the urge to cover my spines in foamy saliva goodness again.

"Know anything about that sign or a **footloose** and **fancy-free** panda?" I asked.

"No," the ringleader said, hiding her hands behind her back. "We've been busy getting our groove on."

Just then, the penguin DJ put on a slow song. Someone turned the lights low, the ring-tails started swaying, and before I knew what hit me, I was rocking back and forth ever so slightly. Just a few more musical notes, and I could rock myself right to sleep.

"Boss," began Vinnie, "are you . . . dancing?"

The lemurs laughed, and my eyes snapped open.

"Don't be ridiculous," I said. "**Hedgehogs don't dance.** This hedgehog, however, does **hunt down hooligans,** and I'm searching for one now."

The ringleader continued to hee-haw, pointing at yours truly. Pretty soon every lemur was laughing and pointing.

We had them right where we wanted.

I pulled out my shiny sleuthing badge. "Excuse me, lemur miscreants," I said. "I need to ask you to put your hands and tails in the air. Please." (A good hedgehog detective never forgets his manners.)

One by one, the lemurs put up their hands and tails.

"Look, boss, they're red-handed!" said Vinnie.

And they were. Literally. I could still make out the dried red paint on their fingers and palms.

Vinnie pulled out a pair of handcuffs, and another, and another. Somehow, he had managed to link them together in a long, tangled chain. "Can't seem to find the key," he said.

CHAPTER 6

"You can put down your hands and tails," I told the lemurs. "This may take a minute." Or two.

"But I did find this," Vinnie announced, holding up a piece of paper. "It's a warrant for your arrest." He shook the paper back and forth, and the ringtails scratched themselves nervously.

I took a closer look at the warrant. It was a receipt for a pair of night vision binoculars and a lie detector machine. I had to give it to Vinnie: The rodent could bluff with the best of them.

"How do you plead?" Vinnie asked. "**Guilty, not guilty,** or **dance contest?**"

There was an enthusiastic murmur among the lemurs at the mention of a dance contest.

"Given the circumstances," I interjected, gesturing to the "**ZOOKEEPER SAYS: Dance!**" sign, "I'd like to remove the third option."

"That leaves guilty and not guilty," said Vinnie.

"**Not guilty,**" said the ringleader.

GEHOG WHODUNIT TURF — DO NOT

CHAPTER 7

I needed some clarification.

"You're all not guilty?" I asked the ring-tails.

They nodded in unison.

"Do you even know the charges against you?" I questioned.

They shook their heads.

"Well, the first charge is obvious," said Vinnie. "**BAD MANNERS.** You didn't invite us to your dance party, and I'm offended."

I was okay being left out of the dance party, but I couldn't overlook the other offenses. "Charge number two: **VANDALISM,**" I said. "You've been using red paint to alter signs throughout the zoo."

It looked like the ring-tails were quaking in their boots. Not that they wear boots.

No boots

Vinnie forged on. "Charge number three: **LETTING THE PANDA LOOSE.** Hopefully, the lug hasn't caused too much trouble at this point."

"Which leads me to your most unforgivable criminal act: **DISTURBING THE PEACE,**" I said. "I haven't been able to sleep in ages!"

"More like hours," corrected Vinnie.

Now was not the time for him to start paying attention to details.

"And don't forget the fifth charge," said Vinnie. "**THEFT.** All those sardines, HipPro cameras, and dance party appetizers came from somewhere."

CHAPTER 7

He dashed back and forth in front of the line of suspects, pausing before each and every one to look deep into their lemur eyes. "And I'd like the recipe for those deviled eggs when you get a chance. They were delish—must have been the paprika."

Vinnie and the ringleader traded secret family recipes on index cards.

My **hedgie senses** went into overdrive when I saw what appeared to be our next clue. "What's this?" I asked, snatching a card from Vinnie's seedy mitts.

"Oh, that's a recipe for **Grandma Gansu's Famous Soup Dumplings,**" explained the lemur leader.

"Who's Grandma Gansu?" I asked.

The lemurs looked like they were all choking on a dumpling at the same time. It was a dumpling made of **deception.**

"Don't know," said Vinnie, "but she must be an extraordinary cook because look how specific this list of ingredients is."

I turned to the ringleader. "Admit it," I said. "The secret to that secret family recipe isn't the ingredients." I paused for effect. (It's what I do best.) "It's that it's not *your* family's recipe."

Vinnie gasped. "I trusted you with my **Great Aunt Vera's Yorkshire Pudding!** I even included the key ingredient: the savory pan drippings left behind by a roasted prime rib."

CHAPTER 7

"The last I checked," I continued, "your troop of lemurs was born and bred here at The City Zoo. Before that, the lemurs came from Madagascar. The only animal native to China, where soup dumplings are from, in these parts is that panda."

"You abducted the panda and stole the key to Grandma Gansu's baking brilliance," concluded Vinnie.

"Or you and the panda are in **cahoots** and planned this dance party together," I chimed in.

"I want to speak to my lawyer," the ringleader stammered.

"Do you have a lawyer?" I asked.

The ringleader shook her head.

"We'll appoint you one," I said. Lou the giraffe was a lawyer on this side of the fence.

"No can do," said Vinnie. "Lou's busy sticking his neck out for justice. Seems the chimpanzees have been wrongly accused."

I pulled out another piece of paper. "Protocol says I need to read you your rights before we take you to jail." (A good hedgehog detective always follows protocol.)

1. You have the right to take a nap anytime and anywhere. If you choose to do so in an abandoned tunnel or compost heap, even better.

2. You have the right to uninterrupted solitude.

3. You have the right to as many worms, beetles, and slugs as you want.

"Excuse me, boss," interrupted Vinnie.

"We don't have time to wax poetic about pickles, herring, or cheese," I said.

"You have the wrong list," Vinnie revealed. "Those are *your* rights."

I glanced down at the list in my hand, and Vinnie was right. Again.

CHAPTER 7

I pulled out another slip of paper, cleared my throat, and started over:

1. You have the right to remain red-paint free. If you choose to repaint another zoo sign, it can be used against you in animal court.
2. You have the right to climb as many trees as you'd like.
3. You have the right to eat an infinite amount of fruit and insects.

The ring-tails seemed pleased with that last point.

We needed to lock up these criminals before they stirred the pot and whipped up any more diversions, although I had a funny feeling they hadn't been doing their own stirring lately.

EHOG WHODUNIT TURF — DO NOT

CHAPTER 8

After we locked up the ring-tails in the big house, we headed back to the dance party at the Lemur Lounge to look for that bamboo-loving bear.

"Look, boss! Over there!" said Vinnie. "It's the **A Capel-LEMURS!**"

I wiped off my glasses. "The A Ca-*who*?"

Vinnie pointed to the stage. "You know, the zoo's *a capella* group. They're a musical act that performs without instruments."

I didn't know but, apparently, I was the only one. Everyone else was wearing A Capel-LEMURS hats and T-shirts and carrying their merchandise.

The crowd was shouting to beat the band. Not that there was a band, but there was a group of indri lemurs singing in sync. I looked to see if they too were red-handed like their ring-tailed relatives, but these lemurs were innocent.

CHAPTER 8

At first, I couldn't be bothered to listen to the A Capel-LEMURS hoot, honk, and hum, but then I almost changed my tune when I realized the primates' percussion wasn't subpar, and their doo-wopping was . . . downright **delightful.** Even their elbow shuffles weren't too shabby. I turned to Vinnie, flapping my elbows ever so slightly. "Where do I get an **A Capel-LEMURS** tote bag?"

"Boss, are you . . . having fun?" Vinnie asked.

"Absolutely not," I replied. "I don't have time for fun." And I certainly didn't have time for fun now that a giant indri was taking the stage. My **hedgie senses** kicked into high gear. The indri is one of the largest living lemurs, but I had never seen one *this* big.

"Who's the **bigwig?**" Vinnie asked, gesturing toward the stage.

"No clue," I replied. There was something about the big primate that didn't jive (and it wasn't the uncoordinated dance moves).

Vinnie helped himself to more bamboo bites, and that's when it hit me: The primate was **too** round, **too** fluffy, **too** cute, **too** cuddly, **too** . . . panda-like! "Vinnie, that's our missing giant panda!"

While my fur-ball sidekick ate his fill, I locked eyes with the supersized singer.

The panda's eyes grew wide. No doubt he realized he was in hot water. He let out an adorable noise—something between a chirp and a honk—and ran offstage and hid.

It was a good ol' game of **hide and seek.** Only the panda wasn't very good at hiding. We closed our eyes and gave him a head start. (A good hedgehog detective always plays fair.) Vinnie started counting to one hundred: "One, two, twenty-three . . . " I had almost drifted off to sleep when he announced, "Ready or not, here we come!"

We found the panda nearby, hiding behind a bush.

Almost.

Then he hid under a table.

Kind of.

And behind a flamingo.

Sort of.

"You're it!" said Vinnie as we cornered the panda near a tree.

The panda, who had managed to walk one of his hind legs up the tree, balanced in a handstand. "Handstands help me relax," he explained.

"Mind if we ask you a few questions?" I asked him, tilting my head sideways.

CHAPTER 8

"Can you make it quick?" he replied. "I have cheese puffs in the oven, and it's important to pay attention to the consistency of the paste, and then I have honey buffalo bites to make, which need to be slow-cooked, as well as mushroom ranch dip and loaded mashed potato bites and homemade cheesy chili to get ready."

It was like listening to my louse-covered sidekick.

"Sorry," said the panda, "I talk a lot when I'm nervous."

Clearly, the cook—and crook—was covering up something.

Vinnie wiped away his thinking-of-cheese drool and pulled out his voice-activated pen that made him prattle on like a pirate. "Time to **batten down the hatches** and begin **Operation Bamboozle.**" He pointed the pen at the panda pooh-bah. "Well, little **lad,** there's been some **scuttlebutt** going around about a missing panda."

"And someone's also been changing signs around these parts," I added.

"That someone," continued Vinnie, "has been **hornswoggling** sardines, HipPro cameras, and gourmet appetizers. And why were you singing **sea chanties** and wearing that ridiculous costume? What say ye, **me hearty?**"

"I don't know what you're talking about," the incognito panda replied. "I didn't do anything criminal. I just wanted to sing and be in a group. Everyone loves my vegetable chop suey, but I want to be known for my singing chops. And it's lonely always being the only panda. I'm innocent until proven guilty, and even if I did do something, which I didn't—" He paused, jumping one hind leg higher and higher up the tree trunk. Nothing about his tree-hugging calisthenics looked relaxing.

"I'd like to **plead the fifth** and remain silent," he continued, still upside down, "that way I'm not forced to testify against myself, and I won't

CHAPTER 8

implicate myself in any funny business—accidentally, of course—even though refusing to respond to questioning could be interpreted as proof that I'm *guilty* because, logically, if I'm *not guilty,* what do I have to hide, right? But that's not always the case because nerves could cause me to frame myself—accidentally, of course—which is exactly why I'm not going to say a word. Starting now."

By the time the giant panda was done, he had practically chewed my ear off. Not that I have big ears.

"You know what we do with uncooperative witnesses?" Vinnie asked.

I wondered if it was the same thing we did with uncooperative sidekicks.

"We turn 'em into **shark bait**."

The giant gymnast dismounted from his tree, and I deducted one point for a wobbly landing.

"So I'm going to ask you again," continued Vinnie. "Someone's the mastermind behind these crimes. Any idea who that **biscuit eater** may be?" He stood on his hind legs and licked his lips. "Wouldn't a fresh, hot-out-of-the-oven biscuit be sublime right about now? Add diced strawberries and some whipped cream, and—**blimey!**—you have the perfect dessert."

"Vinnie, focus," I warned.

"Right, boss," he replied. He turned back to the panda. "*Bear* in mind we can also issue you a ***subpoena.***"

The panda looked both confused and concerned.

"It's like a sub sandwich, only not as delicious," Vinnie said.

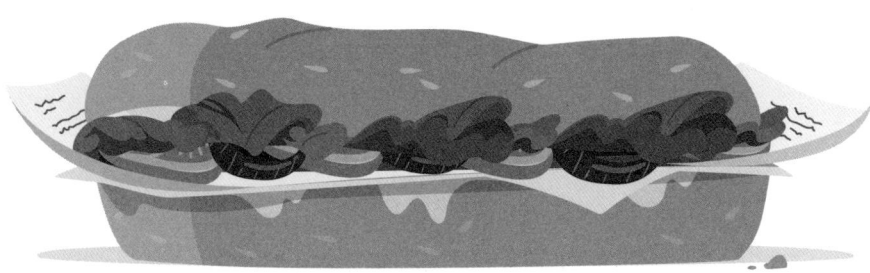

CHAPTER 8

"It's a written document that orders you to appear in **animal court**," I corrected before Vinnie droned on about delicatessen meat.

I'm not sure what the panda pooh-bah was more afraid of: court orders or sandwich orders. Either way, he let out another adorable chirp-honk.

It looked like I could kiss my next nap goodbye.

...EHOG WHODUNIT TURF — DO NO...

CHAPTER 9

After checking his cheese puffs, the panda accompanied us to the big house.

"This is the big house?" he asked, looking around. "It's just the wolf enclosure."

"No lip from you. I'm in charge here," I said.

But the panda pooh-bah was spot-on. Lucky for us, the wolves were preoccupied.

While the panda busied himself preparing honey buffalo bites, Vinnie brought in our prime suspect, the lemur troop's proud leader.

I leaned back on my rock while the lemur made herself comfortable on the rock opposite me. Her long tail swung back and forth. Back and forth.

It was hypnotic, so hypnotic I was dozing off even with my eyes open. I bet this was all part of the primate's plan. She had something up her sleeves. Not that she has sleeves.

"What's swinging?" I asked.

The lemur shrugged.

"Well, you're a barrel of monkeys," said Vinnie, scurrying back and forth between the cave's entrance and my rock.

"Lemurs aren't monkeys," I clarified, "although they are in the same order."

But Vinnie wasn't interested in animal classification. He pulled out a pad of paper and his malfunctioning pirate pen. "Here's the deal: Tell me where ye were this morning, and I won't make **ye walk the plank, ye scallywag.**"

I had to give it to Vinnie: The rodent never gave anyone the runaround, although he was running around the den. Literally. I almost confused him for a hamster.

CHAPTER 9

"I told you already," said the ringleader, avoiding eye contact. "I was getting my groove on in the Lemur Lounge. There's nothing criminal about a little **dance party.**"

I tried a different tactic. "Let's talk about the signs that have been changed around the zoo. What do you know?" I asked.

"Like I said before, I know nothing."

"Nothing?" Vinnie repeated. He got in the lemur's face (almost—even on his tiptoes he was a few feet short) and pointed his pen at her red palms. "Then how do you explain those?"

The lemur looked down at her hands. "Punch preparation for the dance?"

"It was good punch," admitted Vinnie, "but *orange* you lying?" He turned to me to explain. "The punch was orange-flavored. And a bit too tangy for my tastes."

I made a mental note. (Of the orange-flavored punch, not Vinnie's delicate palette.)

"Plus," said Vinnie. "We watched you change that sign in the hippos' home and then escape, paint bucket in hand, through the Woodland Garden, around the Snack Shack, past Zookeeper Zone and the carousel, and into the Lemur Lounge."

Vinnie wasn't exactly telling the truth. It was more of a half-truth. Okay, there was no truth to it at all, but I wasn't about to get into a debate about semantics. We were only minutes away from hearing our felon fess up to her crimes, which meant I was only minutes away from a long overdue heavenly nap.

"I know you're lying," I said. "You've been avoiding eye contact this entire time."

"Which means you're **G-U-L-T-Y!**" said Vinnie, writing it on his pad. He cocked his head to the side as if something weren't right.

CHAPTER 9

It wasn't. Poor distractible Vinnie; he couldn't focus long enough to spell correctly if his rodent life depended on it.

The lemur leaned over. "I think you're missing an 'I.'"

Vinnie did some scribbling. "I mean you're **G–U–L–T–I–E.**" Scribble, scribble. "No, I mean—"

"You mean I'm guilty, which I am," said the lemur. She grabbed Vinnie's pen with her tail and rewrote the word for him. "**G–U–I–L–T–Y.**"

"Yes!" shouted Vinnie. "Time for **Operation Come Clean!**"

Only then did the lemur realize what she had done and hung her head in defeat.

GEHOG WHODUNIT TURF — DO NOT

CHAPTER 10

"You got me," the ringleader admitted. "We made an agreement with the panda that if we let him loose, he'd cater our dance party, and no one turns down Grandma Gansu's famous soup dumplings. We were just having a little fun."

"Yeah," said Vinnie, "You were having so much fun the penguins are sick to their stomachs from all that fish, the hippos' heads are bigger than their bodies from all that fame, and *this guy* over here is so overtired, it's like walking around with a **pet rock.**"

I'm not sure where Vinnie was coming from with that pet rock comment. "Did anyone else help you create all this fun?" I asked.

"If you talk, we'll cut your sentence in half," Vinnie added.

The lemur nodded. "The other ring-tails helped. It was my idea, but they jumped in. They changed the signs, and I handled the spelling."

"And the penguins, hippos, and lions?" asked Vinnie, referring to his list of suspects.

"The hippos were in charge of party promotion and the penguins did the DJing," said the ringtail. "Like you deduced, we were in **cahoots.** Here's proof." She pulled out an envelope and a piece of paper and handed them over.

So AL wasn't sending the hippos fan mail after all. The lemurs were sending them party invitations.

CALLING ALL ANIMALS!
LET'S HAVE A WILD DANCE PARTY To CELEBRATE WORLD LEMUR DAY!

"There's a World Lemur Day?" asked Vinnie. His ears lost their perk. "When's World Rat Day?"

CHAPTER 10

"Based on the number of goodies you just gorged, I'd say it's also today," I replied. "Now let's get back to those lions."

"They were framed," our culprit confessed. "They don't know anything about any of this. You can ask them yourselves."

"We will," I replied. Right after my nap.

"What happens now?" asked the criminal.

"We take your photo, get your fingerprints, and then you'll serve time in jail," said Vinnie.

"For how long?" she asked.

"Depends," Vinnie said. "Four vandalized signs, one emancipated panda, a colony of sick penguins, a herd of haughty hippos, thousands of dollars' worth of stolen goods, and an infinite amount of chaos? You're looking at one to two."

The lemur gulped, "Years?"

"Days," I corrected, which was just long enough for me to squeeze in that nap. "Plus some community service."

"Someone will need to change the signs back to the way they were, convince that panda to head back to his place, and clean up the penguins' pool, the hippopota*mess*, and the Lemur Lounge," said Vinnie.

The lemur and her primate pals could probably get out sooner on good behavior, but I wasn't about to mention that. I needed all of those precious forty-eight hours for beauty sleep. **Every last second.** "The panda, penguins, and hippos will most likely be let off with a warning," I added.

"And you'll give me more of your family recipes when I'm out?" the ringleader asked Vinnie. "I'm going to change my lawless ways and get back to baking. I want to make Grandma Gansu proud."

"You have my word," said Vinnie. "And soon you'll have the step-by-step instructions for the world's best pumpkin cheesecake with a gingersnap crust."

EPILOGUE

And so the ruse is over, I'm back in the homey confines of the **Hedgehog Hut**, and I've hung up my shiny detective badge for the time being. Perhaps I'll crack open another case in a year or two. Or three. No need to rush into things.

Most importantly, we have some peace and quiet around here.

No more sign-changing shenanigans, **no more** sardine-throwing, **no more** selfie-taking, **no more** rouge pandas in the kitchen, and **no more** dance-partying, which is—

Vinnie barged back into my grassy office, out of breath. "Boss, I just got word the wooden cheetah on the zoo's carousel has disappeared."

"I'll get right on it," I said. "**After my nap.**"